The Cousteau Society

SEALS

LITTLE SIMON

Published by Simon & Schuster

New York   London   Toronto   Sydney   Tokyo   Singapore

THE HARP SEAL

Mammal

Weight and size
Baby: 15 pounds, 3 feet
Adult: 375 pounds, 6 feet

Lifespan
30-40 years

Food
Fish and squid

Reproduction
11 months gestation
Baby sheds its coat completely one month after birth.

Lives in northern polar and subpolar regions.

A protected species.

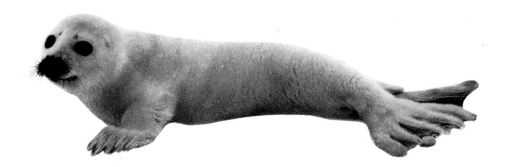

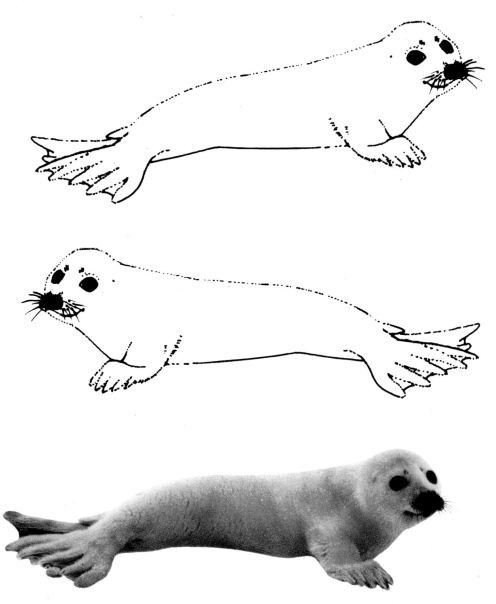

Here are baby harp seals, with their huge black
eyes and white fur.

Heads down! Their white fur helps them hide

from enemies. White on white, unseen, out of sight.

They play together in the snow

while mother seals watch nearby.

Too young to swim,

the pup crawls to its mother.

The small seal uses its flippers like hands

to grab the ice.

It slips, slides, gets wet and hungry. In one month, when

it sheds its white coat, it will be able to swim at last.

The mother seal hears her pup's cry. She knows its

smell. She will feed and protect it until it is old enough to be on its own.